*The Antibody*

Julio José Ordovás

# THE ANTIBODY

## A NOVEL

Translated by Christian Martin-Roffey

**DALKEY ARCHIVE PRESS**

Originally published in Spanish as *El Anticuerpo* by Anagrama in 2014.
Copyright © 2014 Julio José Ordovás
Translation copyright © 2016 Christian Martin-Roffey
First edition, 2016
All rights reserved

[Library of Congress Cataloging-in-Publication Data]
Names: Ordovás, Julio José, 1976- author. | Martin-Roffey, Christian,
    translator.
Title: The antibody : a novel / Julio José Ordováss ; translated by Christian
    Martin-Roffey.
Other titles: Anticuerpo. English
Description: First edition. | Victoria, TX : Dalkey Archive Press, 2016.
Identifiers: LCCN 2016006314 | ISBN 9781943150045 (pbk. : acid-free paper)
Classification: LCC PQ6715.R67 A8413 2016 | DDC 863/.7--dc23
LC record available at https://lccn.loc.gov/2016006

This book was partially funded by the Illinois Arts Council, a state agency.

This work has been published with a subsidy from the Ministry of Education, Culture and Sport of
Spain.

Dalkey Archive Press publications are, in part, made possible through the support of the University of
Houston-Victoria and its program in creative writing, publishing, and translation.

Dalkey Archive Press
Victoria, TX / McLean, IL / London / Dublin

www.dalkeyarchive.com

Printed on permanent/durable acid-free paper

Spit on me as you pass
By the place where I laze.
A sticky reminder
Of life, and the need for rage.

Lois Pereiro

# 1

THE BELLS TOLLED. My mom turned off the kitchen stove and looked out of the window. My neighbor, coming out of the chicken coop, started talking with her. They conferred with each other about the deceased's identity. That which comes from the earth, must return to it. The old man ringing the bell has buckteeth. They call him Serio. My mom would always say that you don't die until your time comes. I don't really get what she meant by it. The neighbor left the coop door open, a carelessness that the chickens took advantage of by venturing outside of it. I ran down the stairs and slammed the door behind me. The clattering latch startled the chickens. My mom yelled at me out the window. The chickens ignored my neighbor's wild hand movements, and I ignored my mother's shouts and the ringing bell as I continued down the street.

# 2

THE SKY HAD already taken off its sweater. A large cloud shaped like dragon wings hunted a smaller one shaped like rabbit ears. The world smelled, sounded, and tasted sweet, just like stolen fruit. We couldn't stay still. The light teased us childishly. We would run around the place busily, looking for trouble and forgetting about our snacks despite our hunger.

Not even birds are born already knowing everything. More than one would have crash landings after their first few flights. We would return the survivors to the rooftops in the hope that their parents would find them before the cats did. The cats, constantly on the prowl, would get their fix torturing them, until they tired of it and killed them. Not to eat them though. They killed just for the sake of it.

The houses had eyes. And ears. And mouths. It was only on the rooftops that we felt free, despite the control that the vultures had over our movements. But for some reason I had trust in the vultures. That is, all the trust you can have in a graveyard watchman.

We didn't get muddy on the rooftops. While those below us prayed, snored, shouted, sighed, moaned, crunched numbers, weaved gossip, and carried out their necessities, we were making Molotov cocktails.

We had more lives than cats, and worse intentions. But it wasn't malice that drove us.

The rooftops were our treasure island. I didn't mind that they'd abandoned me, like they'd done with Ben Gunn. Nor did the solitude scare me, nor the foul angels intimidate me.

The most absurd things ended up on rooftops, just like in canals. The wind amused itself by stealing underwear from the washing lines and placing it on the church's rooftop. Attached to the church was the priest's house, with a little garden in the back. I was surprised when I saw that where once weeds had been growing there were now sky-blue flowers.

The previous priest, just like God in the Old Testament, had resorted to using fear to earn respect. With the new one came an end to his dictatorship. He would absolve us of our venial sins with a simple smile. And he didn't have halitosis, nor hair in his ears.

He wouldn't let us call him Mr. José Luis. There was nothing hidden behind his eyes when he looked at us or spoke to us. He would wrinkle his nose, like a rabbit, whenever his head was in the clouds. His irreverent shirts, clashing with his predecessor's grim mourning attire, had caused quite a stir. The magpies went from bewilderment to annoyance. Not only did he not eat meat but he also rejected warm welcomes. The strangest thing was that, whenever he crossed himself, he would start cackling at the choir!

He took solace in his garden. My mom would say that plants show more gratitude than people. I don't know whether he spoke to the geraniums like she did or if he prayed to them. At the end of the day he would light a pipe and sit down to read. But the telephone wouldn't leave him in peace, and so the book and pipe remained on the chair till the following evening.

# 3

THE DIFFICULT PART wasn't getting in, but getting out.

Every house has its weak point, it's just a case of finding it. Cats and flies were my mentors. The terrace doors and balconies would barely put up a fight. Trees were usually a great help, a branch or two made the journey straightforward. Night wasn't necessarily a good ally. After dinner hour, any type of noise was suspicious.

The old Pantaleon had the dangerous habit of smoking in bed, and one night, before he had put out his cigar, he closed his eyes and never opened them again. During his funeral, the church's saintly scent mixed with the smell of burned flesh, and the rebellious candles created disturbing reflections on the coffin. Later, I managed to sneak into his house through the only crack that allowed in light and air. I didn't have any matches and it took my eyes a while to get used to the darkness. That was another reason why I envied cats: they didn't need matches. A small photo, worn away at the edges, had managed to save itself from the fire. I hid it on top of the wardrobe. My mother always found everything I tried to hide, and I never saw it again.

I got my hands on a lantern. The shopkeeper's daughter would always look the other way whenever she noticed that I was stuffing something into my pockets.

The Germans' house was my secret library. I would take all the books I liked and returned them whenever I felt like it, and often not at all. The Germans were in fact Spaniards who had emigrated to Germany. They would come back to the village every summer with a load of new books. I swear that it was just to piss me off, but each time they would bring more books in German and with less illustrations.

The doctor's place didn't smell like your typical village house. The wind, playing with the curtains, nearly frightened me to death. Locked and on the ground floor was the examination room. There were at least another two rooms on the top floor that were also locked. I tried using all of my lock picks but never managed to open them. That night I dreamed that the doctor's son, while flapping ridiculously like a bird, jumped out of his window and died, strung across the railing.

The houses were filled with echoes and shadows that fought amongst themselves.

In search of unsolved mysteries, I delved into personal affairs.

The teacher's house was about as welcoming as a tomb. The sink couldn't hold any more dirty plates, but the pungent scent didn't just come from the kitchen. There were rotting apple cores in all the corners of every room, even in the toilet. In a small booklet with missing covers the teacher kept a record of the clothes that an old spinster, who hadn't even reached the age of forty yet, had washed and ironed for him. He called her "La Manca," not because she was missing an arm but because she was the daughter of "El Manco." Inside the booklet was a number he had jotted down and I called it a few times. A girl my age would answer in French. I couldn't understand her, and even if I could have, I wouldn't have known what to say. After two minutes, she'd sigh and hang up. I fell in love with her voice and, fantasizing, I immediately drew her a face and gave her a name: Marguerite. My first loves were all imaginary. I would name them all after flowers. From the prefix I figured out that it was a Canadian number. I memorized all of the information about that silent country from the encyclopedia that my mother, without consulting my father, had bought in installments.

The priest's home continued to smell like a sacristy despite the change in ownership. The saints and virgins remained spread out around the rooms, waiting for Judgment Day. José Luis had taken it upon himself to resuscitate the house by carefully painting the walls. I bumped into a bucket and the paint spilled, irreparably, all over the floor tiles. I had to think of something quick. Searching in the garden I found some cat feces and left it in plain sight next to the bucket. Once I was back home I washed my hands and congratulated myself for my deed.

The priest who replaced José Luis had a mouth that smelled of rotten eggs. I didn't like him. I thought it was my fault that José Luis had abandoned the village.

A car arrived early one morning. Someone, overhearing it, rushed to the window and managed to make out two human shadows. On the following day the gossiping buzzed like a cloud of enraged mosquitos.

José Luis kept his mouth shut till Sunday. The old men took their berets off as they entered the church, leaving their bald alabaster heads uncovered. The church was packed and it was extremely hot. The fans seemed to whisper anxiously as they waved in front of people's faces. He looks like a corpse, someone said. True, he did, only the dead don't sweat like that. The Virgin suffered with pity as she watched his glasses slip down his nose repeatedly. Finally, he closed the Bible and took off his glasses. The fans stopped moving and fell silent. I have brought with me a sick person and will take him in at my home as long as is necessary, he said with an authoritarian flourish. And without any further explanation, he asked that we pray for the man and then continued with mass.

The magpies clambered up the walls, uncontrollably irritated. Foreigners would bring out the worst in them. José Luis tried not to lose his composure as he struggled to avoid the birds pecking at him.

# 4

THE MAGPIES SCREECHED as, on Saint John's eve, the sky came falling down. It was God's punishment. There wasn't a flower left standing in the priest's garden. José Luis, with bloodshot eyes, caressed the corpses. At least his book had survived the stone shower. He held it tightly in his arms. Affectionately, he promised to never again abandon it to the elements. Then he blew the water out of his pipe emphatically. He smiled before throwing it on the roof. I took it home with me. Even though I couldn't get it to work, I liked to suck on it and frown, just like I'd seen writers do, as I wrote my first, terrible poems under the moonlight's spell.

If he could stand then it wouldn't be long till he poked his snout out. Since I had nothing else to do, every evening at around seven or when the sun would hide its daggers I would go up to the rooftops and hide behind a chimney. The birds would tweet at the clouds. I'd examine their flight patterns closely. That's how I learned to write, by watching them as they flew.

# 5

I SWORE THAT I had never seen the sea. He didn't believe me.

I have the sea in here, he said while pointing at his head. The sea knows my name and speaks to me like no one else has ever done, but that doesn't mean I always understand it. My father would take me to the seaside some Sundays. We would have a walk round the harbor, listening to the wailing of the boats that had been moored up for too long, and afterwards we'd go to the beach. A muddy beach that smelled of iron, gasoline, dead fish, and rotting seaweed, an end-of-the-world type of smell. He'd carry the cooler by his side and I'd run around him with the same stupid excitement that dogs have when they run around their owners. Afterwards, my father would sit down to smoke and drink beer and I would observe how the crabs and seagulls fought each other. Other times, I'd search for buried treasure in the waste that had been washed up on the shore. The sky wasn't blue, nor was the sea. To be honest, it seemed more like a sky of pus and a sea of ash. We would eat the sandwiches that my aunt had made for us and, before leaving, I would throw the empty bottles into the sea and bury the silver coins I had made from the aluminum foil in the sand.

Got a cigarette?

I gave him a cigarette. He packed it down by tapping it lightly on his knee.

One night, on our way back from the beach, the car went off the road and did a few barrel rolls. I wasn't scared, I swear it: I had my dad with me.

The car wheels wouldn't stop spinning in the air.

Anyone else would have stopped drinking after the accident, but my father, he stopped driving.

He lit the cigarette. He would leave them lit until they almost burned his fingers and then stub them out by grinding them on the sole of his boot. I tucked three or four away into my shirt pocket and offered him the rest of the pack.

The shopkeeper's daughter didn't just turn a blind eye whenever I went into the shop. She would step out from behind the counter and, playing dumb, come right up to me, turn her back, and invite me to touch her ass. She wasn't very pretty, but she had a nice ass.

I couldn't stand the cloudless metallic skies. I was scared they'd collapse.

Doesn't it ever rain here?

Hardly ever, I told him.

When most people think back to their childhood, they think of sunny days. I don't, he muttered.

He stretched out one hand and cracked the nicotine-stained fingers. Then he stretched out the other and did the same. It wasn't the first time I'd seen someone do that, but his bones made a different sound, like glass cracking. His skin was the same color as apples beginning to rot.

Our eyes are made of water, not fire. That's why you never get tired of contemplating the sea and the rain. But I remember the rain being black and sticky. The clouds that the factory chimneys puked out crowded together in the sky like heaps of dirty laundry. The sky smelled like how I imagined a battlefield to smell a week after fighting. It never stopped raining. My aunt warned me to be careful with the rain; she said that it burned. And it did. It burned your eyes, skin, and even your conscience.

My father hated umbrellas. Instead he wore a batwing raincoat with so many holes that it made him look like a gangster who'd been shot up.

# 6

THERE WASN'T A day that went by where he didn't ask me about my mother. If she went to the hairdresser every day, if she called me by my first name, if she was a good cook, if she sang as good as she cooked, if she forced me to eat fish, if she had stopped telling me stories, if she still kissed me goodnight, if she scolded me systematically or only when I did something worthy of it, if she was still in love with my father, if she worked like a mule, if she prayed, if she read and what she read, or even who she voted for. Those kind of questions.

And what does she smell like?

Like how all mothers smell, I suppose, I replied.

I don't know how mothers smell, he said. Do they smell like wet soil? Or dried flowers? Bread? Or mandarins? Detergent? My mother worked in a canning factory and, no matter how hard she scrubbed her hands and washed her clothes, she never managed to get rid of the smell of raw fish. My aunt was always surprised that she was so willing to go to the fishmonger. She hated it whenever I refused to try the fish. Whenever I caught the scent of fish it would always take me over to the corner where most of the cobwebs of my memory gathered. To that place where my mother would gut the baby-sized cod. I couldn't see or hear her, but I could still smell her. Whenever I looked at the fishmonger's wife, it would put him on edge and with a sneer he'd say: What's wrong with you? Are you an idiot or something? They worked together side by side as I twiddled my thumbs, waiting for my turn to be served by her. She wasn't young anymore, nor was she really that pretty or particularly friendly. Her face was gaunt. She had witch-like hair and bags under her dull eyes. Whenever I dreamed about my mother, it was the fishmonger's wife who took her place in my dreams. I'd never get tired of kissing her scaly skin.

My aunt, bored, would claim that my mother was just like me. That no one could get her out of there. And what am I like? I'd ask. Just like your mother, she'd reply.

My aunt would talk about my mother as if she'd been buried for centuries. The strange thing was that I too spoke about her as if she were dead. There was nothing left of her at home, not even her aroma or her reflection. My father had made sure of that. One night, a loud noise got me out of bed. I went out to the hall and into the living room as my aunt shouted: Stop right there! Too late: a piece of glass had already embedded itself in my foot. In one swipe my father had destroyed the coffee set that had been gathering dust on the bookshelves. Something had reminded him that they'd been a wedding present. He'd gotten up off the sofa and smashed them to pieces. My aunt bandaged my foot, up to the ankle; she always made a big deal out of things. Then, emotionless, she swept up the pieces of glass.

You've worn me out. Ask your father.

But I didn't dare ask my father anything, not even the time. It wasn't that she was braver than me. Whenever she was around my father she would bite her tongue and only talk about the weather, the neighbors, or about how expensive things were getting. She'd be the one who'd talk, because her brother wouldn't ever open his mouth.

These two think I'm some sort of servant, she'd complain when my father was out of earshot.

She wasn't our servant but she acted like it. She'd iron our socks and underwear. There was something particularly satisfying about putting on freshly ironed underwear.

Whenever she'd talk about how my father and I were leading her down the road to bitterness, she wouldn't say it with malice.

I remember how her hands would jump about on the tablecloth, nimbly picking at the left over breadcrumbs from dinner. She was the one who cooked, waited on the table, collected the dishes, and then washed them. My father would light up a cigarette and my aunt would bring him the ashtray, a bottle of cognac, and a clean glass that had turned cloudy from all the scratches over the years.

My aunt would sew so that I'd never go without anything. Not once did she say that she'd finish something tomorrow. There was always a skirt for her to sew, a shirt to be ironed, or an omelet for her to turn over, and she wouldn't leave until all those things had been taken care of.

She'd leave her bedroom while tying the belt of her bathrobe a few minutes before my father's alarm clock rang, and I would wake up with the sound of oil crackling in the frying pan. She wouldn't make herself breakfast. She was just fine with the eggs that my father left on his plate and the milk I left in the mug.

Over time she shrank as the bathrobe became bigger around her and the printed flowers lost their petals. She'd dye her hair the color of eggplants. Whenever she sewed, she'd use a pair of glasses that she inherited from her mother, held together with tape. Every day she'd ask me to thread the needle. That's all she'd ask me to do for her. I made her believe that I could thread the needle with my eyes closed.

For a while I started writing my mother's name in the condensation on the windows. My aunt would erase it with the sleeve of her bathrobe before my father would see it and smash his fist through the glass.

Even though they were brother and sister, they had little

in common. When they were young, however, they were like
two peas in a pod. Or that's what she'd say. My aunt kept
her photos in an envelope that had "Family" written on it in
trembling letters. Every New Year's Eve, after the bells had
rung, she'd take it out and place the photos on the mantelpiece that was reserved for special occasions. She'd arrange
the photos neatly, mix them up again, then rearrange them
again, just like she did with the cards whenever she played
solitaire. My auntie must have been the only person in the
world who didn't cheat when playing solitaire.

Has your father wished you a happy birthday? she'd ask
me whenever it was my birthday. I'd lie and say he had. It
was tradition for my aunt to burn the cake. I'm sure she did
it on purpose. It's still edible, she would say as she scraped
off the burned parts.

My aunt wouldn't buy me gifts; instead she'd give me a
brand new, freshly printed banknote. Smell it and you'll see,
she'd say. I'd pretend to blow my nose with the bill and my
aunt would humor me by pretending to get annoyed. With
my brand new bill I'd go to the best bakery in the city. I'd
buy as many chocolates as I had years and treat myself to a
cake. I could spend up to twenty minutes trying to decide
which cake to have, much to the displeasure of the irrita-
ble shop assistant. No one could imagine the happiness I
felt while devouring the cake in front of the luxurious shop

windows. My aunt would bring her hands up to her face when I showed up later that evening with a cream mustache and a little bag of chocolates tied shut with a red string.

You'll never amount to anything if you don't think about your future, she'd tell me with her mouth full of chocolates. I did think about the future. But I wondered what the point was of saving money when you could just rob a bank or a bakery.

My father only ever gave me one present, and you could barely call it that. He saw a robot one day, abandoned on the sidewalk, and brought it home. The dented robot had a life of its own. It would wake up whenever it felt like it, often early in the morning, and go around my room, scanning every corner with its laser vision. My aunt immediately grew fond of it and would clean the dust off it as if she were gently wiping sweat off its forehead.

My aunt had an uninteresting smell, but a homely one nevertheless, like some lost shack in the snow. A shack where a traveler, on the brink of exhaustion, stops and finds a rejuvenating fire, a pot of warm soup, and a hunchbacked peasant woman dressed in rags who asks no questions and tends to his fever with poultices.

She was obsessed with fevers. Right after breakfast, as well as just before going to bed, without fail, my aunt would put the thermometer in her armpit and write down her temperature in what seemed like a never-ending book-let. Since I tended to break the thermometers, occasionally without actually meaning to, she gave up monitoring mine.

# 7

José Luis would make fun of me. But it's just a barn owl, he'd say. A barn owl that has acquired the habit of somehow getting into the church every night. The creature wants to speak with God and ask him for an explanation, but God pretends to be deaf and the big ugly bird is stubborn. We should kill it, I suggested. But he said that we couldn't because the owl had taken sanctuary there.

He passed his fingers over his eyebrows. He'd do that sometimes.

José Luis couldn't hurt a fly, much less a creature like that. Can I tell you something?

The time that my Dad caught me shooting at my next-door neighbor's chickens I got a good beating. With each smack I swore I'd never touch the air rifle again. I saw him coming, his bald head bobbing along the garden wall. I wanted to run, but once again my legs wouldn't listen.

Four or five years had passed since then, which was more than enough time to break a promise.

The rifle was still there. I got rid of the cobwebs and put it in a sack and hid it on the neighbor's roof. I felt important. I had a mission to accomplish.

Shooting at cats and chickens was all good fun. In fact, it was extremely entertaining. But shooting at an owl . . . No one survives its cursed glance.

Owls eat anything they can swallow. I learned that by examining their excrement. That was more instructive than any of the puzzles at school.

The owl had set up its lair in the cursed house, not too far away from the priest's. It would go up to the bell tower and bathe in the full moon's bright light.

That night the moon was blue, red, and purple as if a child or an insane person had painted it and left out the stars. I jumped onto the roof and seized the rifle, then headed to my neighbor's chicken coop. The chickens dreamed of endless fields of corn and romantic fights between roosters. I smiled and my fangs glimmered.

I returned the rifle to its place and carried the dead chicken, which I had put in the tightly shut sack, over my shoulder. As I had imagined, he didn't dare open the sack. You're a man of your word, he said. He wasn't sure how to thank me. We dug a hole in the garden and buried the sack. He opened two bottles of Coca-Cola and we drank and smoked in silence. His arms and legs shook so badly it seemed like he had dug a tunnel to the center of the earth with a spoon.

I know what I can give you, he said. He went inside the house. I heard him rip a sheet of paper. Here, he said. An enormous owl was pouncing, with open wings and outstretched claws, on a small and frightened rat. Both of the animals had human faces. Without a doubt, he was the rat. The owl must have been his father, I suppose.

Two days later, he begged me to dig the owl up and take it as far away as possible. Its cries, now that it's dead, are even more terrifying, he said distressed.

My mom didn't like the drawing.

Where did you get it from?

It's mine, I told her.

But my mom had a lie detector.

# 8

SOME RAN TO be the first to get to school. Others, like me, put off the inevitable for as long as possible. I remember the walk to school better than school itself. We lived on the fifth floor and I would go down each morning counting the stairs out loud, but if one day there were sixty-six, the next day there'd be sixty-five or even sixty-one. Our street was long and narrow with the smell of vomit in the mornings. Strangely enough it was called "Fortune Street." It was worth getting up early in the morning just to watch how the first light of day would fight the leftovers of the night. The shadows, harassed by the street sweepers, would grumble as they returned to the sewers. When it opened its mouth, the city roared and yawned at the same time. My aunt would watch me from the window till I disappeared out of sight. There were repair shops everywhere for cars, motorbikes, bikes, shoes, pants, ovens, fans, lamps, jewelry, frying pans, mattresses, guitars, music boxes, rifles, toys. By the entrance of a watch repair shop, tied to a streetlight, was a dog dying of boredom that would only bark at me. The watchmaker was a hunchback with delusions of grandeur. He'd wear armless glasses that looked like they were made of gold—who knows, maybe they were—as he dissected the watches.

Alarmed by the barking, the hunchback came running out with his leather apron that went down to his ankles and would try, in vain, to calm his dog. They'd both look at me as though I were the Devil himself. I'd throw a diabolical smile back at them and continue on my way, dribbling past various imaginary players with my imaginary ball.

The pigeons also feared my feints and my lethal attacks from the wing.

If I had time to spare I'd take a little detour and go through the abandoned factory that was a refuge for tramps. I didn't feel sorry for them, nor did they frighten me; they just made me feel a little sick. They'd get drunk, insult and beat each other, but they didn't hurt anyone.

There was a completely bare, ancient and lonely tree that appreciated my caresses by answering with a slight tremor. Poor stump. Coffin wood.

I'd be the last to arrive at school and would sit in the back row next to the dirtiest window. The teacher would wave his hands, write on the board, open and close his mouth, and I'd just watch. The black, polluted rain would call to me from the other side of the glass that had been dirtied by all the fly dung. I'd think about my mother, or just stare blankly ahead till the teacher cleared the board and noisily blew his nose, finally signaling the end of class.

At night my aunt would worry that my father would go out to get cigarettes and not come back. So, whenever he ran out of them, no matter how late it was, I'd have to go buy him a pack of Winston. I'd put my coat on over my pajamas while my aunt took the exact change out of her purse. The stairs were in an even worse mood than in the mornings and I had to be careful about where I stepped so that I didn't wake what was lurking in the shadows. There were a few floors where the lights didn't work. Walking in the dark is even harder than walking through fire, but I had a trick. With the coins in my hand, I'd go through all the streets, carefully inspecting the doorways.

I wasn't strong enough to open the bar door. The barman would laugh as I wrestled with it, before coming out from behind the bar while drying his hands with a grubby cloth. Sometimes he'd offer me a Coca-Cola and I wouldn't turn it down. There was a woman at the end of the bar, flipping through a newspaper without looking at the pages, who could've been my mother. Two or three old men were smoking, their eyes fixed on the television. The evening news would either be about the deaths and damage caused by the most recent terrorist attack, or an inaccurate weather fore-cast for the weekend. The barman would give me the pack of Winston and put the coins in the cash register without counting them. When the woman, the one who could have been my mother, got to the last page of the newspaper, she signaled to the barman to fill up her glass.

My aunt would welcome me back with a menacing glare. Your father gave up waiting for you, she'd say. The Coca-Cola would keep me from sleeping. At midnight I'd hear my father get out of bed, go past the bathroom, and into the kitchen to light a cigarette. The minute he went back to bed, my aunt would come out of her room and open the window to let the smoke out. But it wouldn't leave.

There was a movie theater in the neighborhood that would show westerns. It managed to stay open thanks to a small, loyal audience of lonely men, like my father. The theater would fill up with smoke and the horses had to pass through that smog after the clouds of dust from the desert. Years later it only showed porn movies. The small audience was faithful till the end, until the theater fired the girl at the ticket office and banned smoking.

Nearly every western starts with a man riding down a long and rocky path trying to escape his past. As the film continues the guy realizes that his past isn't history and that his destiny's already been written. I don't think my father thought about that. He'd get more excited about gunshots and fistfights and was a firm believer in vigilante justice.

When a man rides aimlessly, he's hiding something.

The Indians didn't kidnap my mother.

It's pretty unpleasant when they kidnap a Comanche woman. But if an Indian takes a woman from a white man, that's much worse, said one cowboy to another as they were giving their horses a drink.

It was pitiful, watching my father shooting at himself in the mirrors.

We'd ride together in my dreams. After overcoming thousands of dangers, we'd arrive at a deserted town where there wasn't even a cockroach left. The bank, hotel, Sheriff's office: everything was empty. We'd go into the saloon and my father would place a bottle of whiskey and two glasses on the bar. He'd pull the cork out with his teeth and fill the glasses up to the brim. Drink, he'd demand. But Dad, I'm just a kid and kids don't drink, I'd reply. My father would then take out his pistol: I told you to drink. The whiskey would burn my throat and the tears would sting as they went down my cheeks.

I felt safer sleeping with a gun under my pillow, even if it was a toy. They would have killed my father before he'd even drawn his gun. He had death sketched on his face.

Someone knocked on the classroom door. Everyone was startled. The principal crossed the room, spoke with the teacher, and then pointed his finger at me, but it wasn't the usual accusatory finger. I followed him back to his office. He let himself fall back into his throne and showed me his large yellow teeth.

Your father's in the hospital, he said.

I must not have reacted as he'd expected.

His shoulders were covered with dandruff. He was the same as all the other teachers in that respect.

Your aunt phoned us, he continued.

He sunk his hand into his pocket and took out some crumpled, faded money.

Get a cab, he said.

Was it his duty as principal to never get rid of his horrible maroon sweater? With the money he'd given me he could have bought himself a new one, maybe a different-colored one on sale. And some anti-dandruff shampoo.

The hospital was far away and it was raining furiously. Even though I realized that one of the soles of my shoes was peeling off, I jumped from one puddle to another in a sudden fit of euphoria. I was free. I had cash. Fallen from the heavens.

Two or three taxis drove by without me doing anything to stop them.

They sold single cigarettes in the arcades. I'd swallow the

smoke like it was saliva and would cough and spit nonstop.
I had noticed that if you wanted to spit with class, you had
to do it casually.

I really was good at pinball. If I wasn't the best, I was
one of them. There were some who thought I could move
the ball with my mind. The machine's lights and music was
entrancing. And that entrancement, which had begun to
change me, was addictive.

No one ever looked at their watch in the arcades. Time
would seem to stand still or last forever, depending on how
good you were or how many coins were in your pocket.

It wasn't raining anymore by the time I went back outside
with my triumphant smile and empty pockets. The rainbow
signaled the way to the hospital.

My aunt was wearing her slippers. She folded the maga-
zine that she'd been using as a fan. My father calmed down
once my aunt had put a wet cloth on his forehead.

The fever wouldn't go down. He spent a month in the
hospital. That's where he became an admirer of books about
the Old West. My aunt's glasses stopped the letters from
making him dizzy.

I'd visit him every evening just for the pleasure of going
up and down the hospital elevator. I found it highly suspicious that the nurses' and doctors' uniforms didn't have any
remnants of blood on them.

My aunt, following the doctors' advice, bought him a walking stick. I'm not a cripple, my father said. He tried to break the stick and, since he couldn't, threw it at the television instead. My aunt said that it wasn't the television's fault and fetched a broom to brush up the pieces of glass.

We spent three or four weeks without a TV. It felt like a family member had died.

# 9

HE DIDN'T USE the same tone that adults used with me. He wasn't condescending, nor did he ever tell me what to do.

How old do you think I am?

. . .

Give me a number.

Fifty?

He howled maniacally with laughter.

How'd you get the tobacco? he asked.

I told him about the shopkeeper's daughter.

Why haven't you fucked her yet? I'll tell you one thing, I'm much happier now that I can't get it up. At your age I always had a hard-on which, apart from being uncomfortable, was extremely dangerous because it blocked the blood flow to the brain.

I stopped stealing comic books and started stealing porn magazines instead. I'd lock myself in the bathroom with them until my aunt, pounding on the door, threatened to call the fire department. I was a horny little bastard. I'd search in the wash for my aunt's dirty panties and smell them. I'd wait for her to fall asleep and then sneak into her room in the dark and get off on listening to her heavy breathing. Once I was sick in bed for three days and broke all the masturbation records.

My friends were much filthier than me. The girls in the neighborhood were scared or disgusted by us, probably both, and would run away whenever they saw us coming. We didn't have a chance with them and so we pooled our money, everyone giving what they could, and drew straws to see who was going to get laid.

You can probably guess who the lucky guy was. One Friday, after finishing school, we went to the neighborhood brothel where I'd seen my friends' fathers go. It was a dump with half a dozen old, fat, and sullen-looking whores. They were smoking and playing cards. My prize came with one condition. My friends got to decide for me and, of course, picked the oldest, fattest, most sullen-looking whore and shoved me over in her direction. The whore, who had a voice like a sergeant's, ordered me to stay put at the bar until she'd finished playing. We laughed at the barman who looked like our literature teacher, only he didn't have a mustache, but a scar that made him look pretty tough. The barman set his henchmen on my friends.

The card game wouldn't end and I was getting light-headed. The barman gave me an empty glass and said to fill it up in the bathroom sink if I wanted to. The sergeant threw down her cards in defeat, stood up and ironed out the creases in her skirt. I hope this little angel has taken his Holy Communion, she joked. The other whores and the barman laughed. I followed her down a hallway that got narrower, darker, and smellier as it went on. We went into a room with a bed, a mirror, a bidet, and a lightbulb that didn't have many minutes of life left. Cash up-front, she demanded. I emptied my pockets onto the bed. What, did you break the piggybank? she growled. A few coins rolled around on the floor. I had to crawl under the bed, where even the socks were hiding in fear. She counted the money. I was two or three dollars short. Only because I feel sorry for you, she said, stuffing the money into her pocket and the loose change into a sequin bag. She'd taken her clothes off before I'd even realized it. Her toenails were painted snake-green and she had a tarantula between her legs. The bidet trembled under the mountain of flesh. Are you cold? I shook my head. Well then, kid, what are you waiting for? Pull down your pants. She washed me with soap. Her motherly hands and the warm water were enough. After she'd realized that she'd finished the job before it had even started she began laughing, first with her hand over her mouth and then cackling out loud.

I would have ripped her eyes out, but the knot in my throat was stopping me from breathing.

I went out onto the street faking victory. My friends crowded round, anxious to find out the details. I'd always been good at exaggerating but that day I outdid myself. We bought red wine and Coca-Cola and went to Anchor Park. I didn't want my friends to suspect anything, so I drank the concoction like it was champagne. That night I was sick in bed. My aunt's cries woke me the next morning. She thought I'd bled out.

We flew like flies, without reason and without leaving the neighborhood. All we had was a park bench and we didn't need anything else to feel like we ruled the world. We fed ourselves with sunflower seeds, beer, and smoke, and spat our fury out at the blood-soaked clouds that infected the skies. Everything tormented us and yet we'd laugh at almost anything. We must have looked like idiots and probably were. We had a good time on our bench, our sides splitting with laughter, and having fun was all that mattered.

We had millions of pimples and, frankly, we smelled disgusting, but we weren't a bunch of lepers like the girls thought we were.

Whenever we weren't fighting, we were clowning around or philosophizing. We had lots to talk about. Important matters, and we wanted the whole world to hear us. We'd carve our names into trees, benches, and lampposts for future generations. We, who had been spat out by society and the system, would vomit that mushy puree of fear, disgust, indignation, and indifference onto the walls.

The park got its name from the years when an anchor had sat rotting at the bottom of the estuary. The only things that would climb the trees were the cats trying to escape domestic tyranny, and the majority of the lampposts were broken. It wasn't much different from a prison yard or an abandoned zoo, but it was the only place where I'd seen the earth scratch at the sky and the sky bite back.

I call it "First Time Park" because that's where I was first punched, where I scored my first goal, and where they passed me my first joint. There was fighting daily. We fought democratically though, everyone against each other. It was a healthy type of violence, even if at times someone would lose a tooth or an eye, break a bone or get their balls crushed. We fought to find our strength and pass the time. The old men would applaud or jeer as they placed bets on us.

It was in that park that I discovered there were only a chosen few who dared to walk on their hands.

I wasn't good at anything, not football, not fighting, and I had the nasty habit of laughing at others, especially the elderly. Actually, I didn't really laugh, I would just smile, but my smile was enough to severely irritate the park thugs, just like it did the teachers—thugs in their own right. I had an honest smile and many people couldn't take it. I couldn't understand why my smile was so provocative and why the powerful few, those with corrupt smiles, weren't prepared to tolerate me threatening their authority. For them, mine was like a threat or an insult.

The Lobster would barely separate his lips; hiding behind them was a set of teeth as crooked as they were rotten. The Lobster thought that all smiles, sneers, and smirks were aimed at him. He was paranoid and had reason to be so: his sister would go around from boy to boy and motorbike to motorbike. She had the body of a blow-up doll and the brains of a mosquito. It was the perfect combination to become the neighborhood's first celebrity, and then, thanks to some practice and a bit of luck, onto becoming a porn star. I thought that she was all right. She was one of the few that greeted me in the street, but that doesn't mean I didn't make fun of her like the rest.

We played the usual teenage games. Like fucking a lamppost and calling it the name of the gym teacher, or the French teacher, or one of the mothers of whoever wasn't there at the time. Once, through laughter and exaggerated moaning, while clinging onto a lamppost I decided to call out the Lobster's sister's name just as he was coming out of the bushes. He charged at me like an enraged buffalo. I should have climbed up the lamppost, that would have been the smart thing to do; but instead I stood there and waited for his assault. I dodged the first and second punches, but not the third or fourth. A crowd gathered around us and the old men took their wallets out. I doubt any were stupid enough to bet on a flea-ridden runt like me against a rottweiler like him. Maybe it was the taste of blood or a burst of rage, or simple desperation, but instead of throwing myself at his feet and begging for mercy or a quick death, I hung onto his neck and severed his ear in one bite. His screams shook the surrounding trees and a shower of black leaves fell on the both of us. I jumped out of the way to avoid being strangled and spat out the piece of ear that I had ripped off. One of the old men began applauding and the others followed.

Everyone there knew that the Lobster had a knife on him. Even I knew it, but in that moment I'd forgotten. He took his knife out, stepped forward and dug his eyes into mine. It was then that I heard my mother's voice. My dear son, was the only thing she said, or the only thing I heard. I stepped forward and the Lobster felt how the knife began to burn in his hand, I could see it on his face; but instead of dropping it he gripped it tighter.

That's enough!

An old man hit the Lobster's hand with his walking stick.

The knife rolled on the ground, spinning around madly, ending up in the mud. The mud, with a life of its own, swallowed the knife up and deprived me of my trophy.

# 10

WHEN THE OWL finally stopped complaining the frogs took its place.

What if we poison the river?

It was an amateur river that only lived up to its name "Living Water" every four or five years and would pounce on its prey while roaring and blaspheming. In summer it would be reduced to a minimal presence. The dead child in the well cried because the tentacles ripped up his fine little sailor's outfit. He went missing the day of his Holy Communion. The bells rang and the whole town, men and women, young and old, went out looking for him. Someone saw a white shoe floating amid the algae.

There was another well with a different dead child, but no one heard his cries.

The frogs would sing in the summer night. Their repertoire depended on the moon's phase, the number of stars, and the tension in the air. I couldn't bring myself to tell him that the frogs that tormented him were the same ones that Huck and Jim heard sing out from their raft on their escape to freedom.

Some build walls just so others can destroy them. That's how the world works. How it's always worked. The walls of the car cemetery were the most terrifying in the neighborhood. They were the tallest and had broken glass across them. We had wings and our skin was as thick as our skulls.

Inside the cemetery we'd look for cassettes that we could sell in the park. The owner was known as the "Bear." However, a real bear would have sensed the intruders invading his territory and looting his supplies.

We'd clean the cars out. I fantasized about finding a gun in a glove box. My dream came true, the same way my dreams always did. I found a lighter shaped like a gun that would have gotten a good price if I hadn't given it to my father, knowing he wouldn't even fill it up with fuel. I gave my aunt a half-filled bottle of perfume that looked expensive. It was a little too adventurous for her. It's the type of perfume that unbridled women wear, she said. My aunt was on the opposite side, the one with all the chained-up, unhappy women.

He may have had a bad sense of smell but the Bear was no idiot. We heard his growling and roaring. One of the group, running on top of the cars, managed to jump over the wall and land in a freshly watered cornfield. Another hid under a car. I locked myself in a car's trunk. The police dog had a better sense of smell than the Bear, as well as fangs that glimmered mercilessly.

A frozen light scratched at the bleak walls of the police station. My friend looked at me, I looked back and we both laughed at each other. A pig-eyed officer threatened to handcuff us. The police gave off the same repugnant smell that teachers did. They would write on the typewriter with two fingers, huffing and blowing out smoke through their ears.

The clouds started to dribble. My aunt's umbrella refused to open and there was no changing its mind. She covered her head with a plastic bag from the supermarket and I pulled my hood over mine. If only you had a proper set of parents like everybody else, she said. Our shadows marched in opposite directions. Mine had already stopped following me, and would never start doing so again.

# 11

I'D BRING HIM packs of cigarettes, cans of Coca-Cola, and bags of sunflower seeds. We'd make two piles from the shells. Two gigantic piles. And we'd laugh when they collapsed.

Take everything out of your pockets.

I'd seen it in films: when they were about to put someone behind bars, the officer would dispossess him of everything and I thought it was humiliatingly cruel.

And what about these stones?

To start fires.

And the pocket mirror?

In case someone's spying on you or you need to send signals by reflecting the sun's light.

And what about this old piece of junk?

It was my grandfather's watch. A pocket watch. I told him what my grandfather had told me. After the war, he ended up in prison and shared a cell with a pickpocket who bragged about having the quickest hands in the whole of Barcelona. To prove he wasn't all talk, he stole the prison warden's watch and gave it to my grandfather. My grandfather spent the next two years waiting to be released from prison with it hid up his ass.

I also told him that they had killed my grandfather the previous summer.

How?

A hit-and-run by some drunks.

He said that we'd hang them together but I replied that I'd be fine with breaking their legs and sentencing them to a life in a wheelchair.

I collected my things. I didn't think it was necessary to show him the penknife I had tucked behind my belt that had gotten me out of a few tight spots.


Even if it's hard, you still have to live life. The amount of times I heard my aunt say that.

They'd given my father the sack. Even without setting the alarm clock, he'd wake up at the same time, sometimes even a little earlier. He didn't shave every day anymore and would barely try the eggs at breakfast. Every so often he'd leave the front door open behind him in the morning.

You can smell the unemployed just like you can old people.

My aunt prayed they'd give him disability benefits.

My father felt like he was someone important in the neighborhood because whenever he walked into a bar he never had to tell the barman what he wanted. My aunt hated barmen. Have you ever seen a barman at a funeral or visiting a patient in a hospital? I told my aunt that whatever she had to say to my father she should say it to his face and to stop being such a pain in the ass.

We needed some headquarters and thought the old factory would be the perfect place. We told the tramps to get lost, but they neglected our invitation. There were fifteen or twenty or maybe even twenty-five tramps there, all of them old, bearded, and drunk. They slept, some on top of others, around a campfire where they'd roast seagulls that they had managed to catch during the evening. We filled a cooking pot with nails, screws, nuts, and bottle caps, topped it up with gunpowder and threw it over towards the campfire while covering our ears. The explosion was immense. The tramps shouted, screamed, and ran around crashing into each other. The mayhem drew the police but the officers didn't even bother to get out of the car.

It was hard work clearing out all the trash. The old factory had been bombed during the war and a few of the bombs dropped on it still hadn't detonated. We weren't able to find them. We laughed as we imagined taking a bomb to the police department. Hey pigs, we brought you a little present! Just like in the cartoons.

We furnished our mansion with a three-legged table, a

few mutilated chairs, and the backseat of a car that had its guts showing. We used the porcelain urinal that the tramps had abandoned during their escape as an ashtray.

We'd be silent for hours, concentrating on the sound of the rain and watching mice race around. I was the only one who could hear the ghost's cries ricocheting off the walls.

A one-eyed dog joined the group. We cleaned him up a bit, deloused him, and filled his stomach with cat food, much more expensive and much tastier than dog food. He had fought with all types of dogs, men, and other monsters. His scars proved that. He would make us laugh whenever he yawned, opening his mouth so wide that he dislocated his jaw. He wasn't like other dogs. He didn't have an owner and he didn't want one either.

He would screw up his snout if he didn't like the way a person smelled. Whenever the police were near he would show his fangs and blood would shoot into his remaining eye. He didn't sleep easy, but it wasn't because of the mice racing around him. He feared something.

It was thanks to the dog that the girls started coming up to us. He would let them stroke him, closing his good eye calmly as they played with him. If any were on their period it would make him crazy. He'd follow them with his tongue out and they would run around pretending to be scared.

He looked happy, probably happier than he'd ever been,

but he was sentenced to following his own path. There were shadows hunting him and he couldn't let them catch him.

# 12

HE TOOK OFF his glasses. Try them on, he said. It didn't matter that they were made out of plastic, they still felt heavy. What do you see? I see a woman with kind eyes next to a window, I told him. A fragmented light filtering through the windows. The woman is holding a fish in her arms. Only it's not a fish. It's a child. Opening and closing its mouth. Now I see another woman. She's sweeping in the desert and singing an age-old song. Now I can see a dog with its nose plunged into a puddle of blood. It's raising its head, it's looking at me, it only has one eye, a human eye, it's licking its lips and now it's put its snout back in the puddle. Now I can see a toilet filled with vomit, the darkest vomit I've ever seen. If I dropped a match into the toilet it would go up in flames. Now I see two girls. Twins. They're playing catch with a head and the head is laughing along with them.

I gave him back the glasses. He put them on like he was placing a bandage.

When I mentioned the girls his hands started to shake nervously.

They were the spitting image of each other and even dressed identically from head to toe. The game consisted in trying to figure out what had changed from day to day. It could have been the earrings, socks, belt, or the ring that one wore on her left hand and the other on her right.

They would both use the same words and as they spoke they would spew and spit them out only to chew them back up again. They would both bite their nails and had the same cold smile. It was impossible to figure out which was the crazier of the two.

This place lacks atmosphere, they said the day they conquered our castle. They brought a cassette player with three or four badly recorded tapes. No one understood a word of English but those dirty songs opened our minds up like they'd been smashed with a hammer.

They would lie to their parents, just like they did with the teachers, us, and even with each other. They showed up one night at the castle, shouting that it was snowing outside. We weren't in the mood to joke around. Five minutes later, however, our curiosity piqued, we abandoned our uninspiring bubble of smoke. It wasn't snow but ash that was falling from the sky. Dancing around under the flakes raining down on them, they began to celebrate the Apocalypse. They left snake tracks on the blanket of ash.

One of them had a birthmark on the left side of her body.

It looked like a cloud and, like clouds, it would change color and shape constantly.

Their father worked in a funeral parlor and had that helpless air about him of a person who's been condemned to wearing clothes that don't fit. Despite that, whenever he looked at you he would instill a sense of tranquility.

The twins had created their own circus where they both performed as trapeze artists, tamers, and clowns. They would swing over the abyss, file and polish the tiger's nails, and mock the audience by tricking them into believing that they were actually ridiculing each other.

They took me to their house once when they wanted to show me something. They lived in the only building in the whole neighborhood that had an elevator. Their apartment was on the second floor. They refused to use the elevator and I went up by the stairs. Under the peephole on the door, there was a tin-plated Christ that warned: *Enter through the narrow gate.* The twins rang the doorbell as if they were using a secret password. Their mother took so long to answer the door that it seemed like she had risen from the grave. At least that would have explained the cobwebs in her hair.

The twins took their shoes off before kissing their mother. I didn't. They would have laughed at my patched-up socks. There was a large collection of hats and caps on the coatrack but I couldn't remember seeing their father ever wearing anything on his head. A chandelier with electric candles filled the hall with shadows.

It's five, we'll have some tea now, said the twins' mother. I'd never had tea before. It tasted like bitter soup so I poured three teaspoons of sugar in it, and then another three. Even the biscuits were bitter, but I was starving so I ate every last one in the box. The twins looked at me, then at their mother, then back at each other and smiled. They didn't try the tea or the biscuits. Half an hour had passed, if not longer, but the clock in the living room still said five to five.

I gave her a light, her lighter wasn't working. Their mother finished her tea quickly and put out the half-smoked cigarette. I have to go now, she said. The twins got up after her.

There was a huge pile of framed photos on the small table that was covered by the leftover material from the curtains. One seemed to have fallen over. As I picked it up I saw the twins' mother. She wasn't much older than her daughters were at the time and she was wearing a nun's habit. Absurdly, I crossed myself and left the photo face down how I'd found it.

Their mother said good-bye to me from the hallway. The twins acted normal again once they no longer sensed the maternal radiation.

Their room was less accommodating than a submarine's cabin. They slept in a bunk bed. The barred windows looked onto the neighbors' patio, which the pigeons had chosen as their burial ground. So that their deaths could be a little sweeter, the twins would open the windows and blast Led Zeppelin's "Stairway to Heaven" at full volume.

There was a box hidden inside another one on top of the wardrobe. Inside they had put their mutilated dolls. Not because they were bored of them, but because they didn't want to hear their cries anymore.

Their parents didn't share the same bedroom. Their mother's room was wallpapered. A red bird with a bent beak threatened us from anywhere we looked.

One of the twins covered my eyes as I opened one of the chest of drawers.

What's that?

An instrument of penitence, they explained.

Their cackles offended the parrot printed on the walls.

You should try it. Maybe you'll enjoy it.

It was a metal cilice.

Purification through pain.

In the drawer there was a set of rosary beads coiled up lovingly on top of a nun's dress.

I lay down on the bed, stretched out my hand, and opened the book that had been resting on the bedside table. It was an old, thick book titled *Slaves of God or Wives of Christ*. The pages were soaked in blood. They would dislocate their bones, rip out their hair and fingernails, tear out their eyes, cut their breasts off, skin them alive, rip their limbs off, rape them, prostitute them, decapitate them, feed them to the beasts, shoot them, burn them alive, but they wouldn't renounce their love, their faith, their madness.

No wonder it aroused me so much, even the twins noticed.

# 13

It was a big day. The twins turned up at the factory with a cheese ball. They had heard that what people said about rats being untamable was a myth. You could tame rats. All that was needed was some insight. And patience.

The twins had come up with a few ridiculous-looking traps. To our surprise, however, in just a few hours we'd caught more than ten rats. But we didn't know where to put them, so we were forced to let them go. We made a cage capable of holding a few dozen rodents and set the traps up again. Once again, the rats took the bait.

They were old, scrawny, and half-blind. Since we didn't have any shampoo we decided to wash them with detergent, and they turned out even more disgusting than before. We then picked out the least repugnant ones and, despite the twins, who were in favor of freeing them, we burned the rest.

The smell of burning rat is deadly.

It's not easy putting yourself in a rat's shoes. You can't reason with rats. There's no point punishing them or hitting them either. You have to stare fixedly into their eyes and whisper vulgarities to them. That's what they like.

Rats are pickier than any other animal when it comes to music. Even though they prefer Wagner they don't mind a bit of punk rock. Standing upright on their back legs, curling and uncurling their long tails frenetically, they would dance like Apaches under the influence of the hashish that we'd sprinkled onto the cheese. They would dance to exhaustion. Even after death, they would still move their legs in the air.

I pleaded with them to listen to me and they just stuck their tongues out. I begged them to leave me in peace, and they crucified me. Who do they think they are? God observes you through them, José Luis told me, but I replied that God should keep his nose out of it. José Luis then filled his pipe, taking his time graciously—he's very theatrical—and offered me some drags. Holy smoke. Blessed be.

I thought that the stars only shone in the past, when men would waste their lives chasing dragons that would nurture their children's dreams and their enemies' nightmares. The moon in my town was flaky and chipped. I was so drunk that I couldn't bear to look at it.

José Luis took me out from inside a trash can and brought me to this rat cage where the stars conspired against me. On the night of the Crucifixion all the stars as well as the moon covered their eyes, ears, and noses. Just like Pilate. I told José Luis how I would have liked to be the Roman who, as an act of mercy, pierced Jesus Christ's heart with a spear. He got even more annoyed when I said they should've wet his lips with Coca-Cola instead of vinegar.

What have I done to the stars? What do they accuse me of? If only I could contemplate them with the eyes of a sailor, a poet, a soldier, or a tramp. But I don't trust their eyelids. The light gives life to the shadows. I don't have the energy to follow the monsters in their games anymore. Playing with monsters is fun, but exhausting.

The blind smile, but the deaf never do. Before my father turned deaf he didn't smile either.

Blindness forces you to trust in others, but deafness makes you suspicious of everyone. My aunt and I wouldn't dare smile in front of my father. We would lower the volume on the TV and each of us would go to our rooms. He would then cross over to the other side of the screen and, once inside, would whirl around like a sock in a washing machine.

Life is made up of a thousand little sounds. Could my father use his memory to hear the whips cracking, or could he no longer hear the gun fights in the westerns?

My aunt would clean up after my father, but it was too much for her to handle alone. A vacuum cleaner, like the ones they raffled out when you opened a savings account, would have made life easier for her. But we weren't lucky enough. We never won anything. Nothing that was worth much anyway. At least that's what she would say, sighing.

She was a true martyr, wife of Christ and my father's slave. I gave her a crucifix I'd found in the cemetery that had fallen off a tombstone. It wasn't made of bronze but it glimmered and weighed like it was. My aunt should have used it to slay the cause of her martyrdom. That was why I gave it to her.

# 14

THE MAYOR'S WIFE fanned her husband. After noticing that his mustache was beginning to fade, she took a handkerchief out of her pocket, dampened it with salvia, and wiped his lips.

José Luis needed an altar boy. He offered me five hundred pesetas. It wasn't a bad deal. The robe was a bit small and itchy, but I basked in my place on the altar, where I could observe everyone without them paying any attention to me.

Jesus believed he could conquer the world and with his helpless army he could transform it. He gathered the weakest and armed them with faith. Although he won a few battles, he knew that the war was lost, but he believed that as a result of his defeat, we would come out victorious.

José Luis was in his element in front of the microphone. Jesus looked at me from the cross, begging me to take the nails out of his hands so he could clap approvingly at the sermon. Even the tears of the Virgin Mother of Sorrows seemed real.

The mayor cursed the breeze that had brought that two-faced being to his village. The similarities between José Luis and Saint Roch had to be more than just pure coincidence.

The plague-infested people were banned from entering the land of the healthy, condemned to wandering the land and sounding a dreary bell while pleading to God to open the gates to the eternal kingdom. Only an insane man such as Saint Roch would have dared to wash their wounds and wipe away their sins. Saint Roch wasn't a superhero like Saint George or Michael. He didn't ride a horse, wear armor, use a spear, or wield a sword, and even the dog that had sworn loyalty to him was a mangy mutt. Saint Roch didn't have superpowers and would distastefully display his ulcerated leg.

The largest celebrations were held in his honor. The magpies had dyed their feathers and gone to get perms. The mayor and his entourage puffed out their chests and sucked in their stomachs. The youngsters had permission to bathe in alcohol. To the rhythm of the paso doble they would sacrifice a calf, shitting itself from fear. The outdoor festival was then completed with a crate of fireworks with the outcast saint's face printed on it.

Unlike his father, who was a master of cruel jokes (so much so that he laughed at Abraham when commanding him to sacrifice his firstborn son), Jesus didn't have any sense of humor. Not once did he joke with his disciples, nor did he let them joke around in his presence. His message would have gotten across better had he included a joke or slipped a hint of irony into his parables. I would have fallen at the feet of a Christ who smiled. But it's understandable that he wouldn't want to smile after having seen, even before being born, his entire life story.

The priests wouldn't wait for the sermon to finish before passing around the hat. It wasn't the amount that people gave, but the way they would throw the money into it. There wasn't a left hand that didn't know what the right hand was doing. What was even more revealing was how they took their communion. Some would open their beaks like chicks, others would stick out their tongues like ruminants, while others held out their hands like beggars.

Mass was a successful business for both of us. José Luis gave me the five hundred pesetas as promised and then another hundred on top of that. He wanted to tell me something, but instead he thanked me and told me that he would see me again soon. He was in a rush.

I blew out the candles, switched off the lights, and sat down to tie my shoelaces. I didn't care if my shoes were dirty, but I couldn't stand my laces being untied. The breathing of the saints was like a relaxing tune. Saint Roch's dog sniffed the flowers that had been left at his owner and lord's feet. There was no doubt that he was blessed. Any other dog would have torn them to shreds.

It wasn't the holy spirit that descended on me but the damned owl, and it nearly scared me to death. Owls slept during the day but this one must have been an insomniac, or maybe it was just sleepwalking. It staggered along the altar like a toy whose batteries were running out. It was then that I saw the red medallion visible on its chest. I thought to myself: It's going to kick the bucket any moment now. But then it took flight and disappeared. It left a few drops of blood on the altar's mantelpiece, I poured candle wax on them so that, if the magpies discovered them, they wouldn't think anything strange had happened.

# 15

Bars near hospitals are almost always depressing. They fill up with lonely people that all chew the same sandwich with the same greediness or exact same loathing. Laughter is contagious, happiness isn't. There's nowhere quite like those bars to observe just how contagious sorrow is. And yet, despite that, a man who drinks and eats alone always seems unhappy. Can you tell the difference between a man who has just had a child and another who has just lost one, simply by the way they scarf down their sandwich or finish off their beer?

A fuchsia shirt, pumpkin-colored pants, and Franciscan sandals. He had to be the one. He appeared to be less gloomy and had put on a bit of weight, especially around his face; he had kept his scruffy beard but not his rebel's quiff or his browline glasses. He was adamant that the girl with Down Syndrome should finish her sandwich; the girl threatened to stab him in the eye with the straw from her drink if he didn't leave her in peace.

I carried on reading the newspaper article about an inter-view with a writer who claimed that the reason he wrote was to stop himself from setting off bombs.

What are you doing?

I told her that I was reading.

Sweetheart, don't annoy the man.

He also recognized me, despite my cap and glasses, and seemed genuinely happy about it.

Long time no see!

In awkward situations the set phrases always come out by themselves.

That's my daughter, he said while rubbing her hair. The girl responded by pulling an annoyed face.

Just because he wore a wedding ring didn't mean that he'd renounced bearing his cross. It was more likely that he'd given up lying to himself.

The girl examined my plate of french fries with a menac-ing sparkle in her eye.

Civilian life had done little to reduce his priestly tics. He would carry on speaking and gesticulating like a priest.

He lived in the outskirts, in a townhouse with a garden. He'd found a seasonal job in a toy factory and was visiting his eighty-year-old aunt who was in the hospital, although he said that it was nothing serious and that she'd be released soon enough. Thank God, he emphasized.

He couldn't hold it any longer and asked me how the village was doing. I told him that the magpies had all the carrion they needed.

The girl had emptied the bottle of ketchup on my fries and was hoping to carry out the same operation with the mustard. I had to stab her in the hand softly, without anyone noticing, to prevent her doing it.

He also knew that Josu's ghost was going to appear, but I never would have guessed that he was about to say what he did.

Whenever I read anything of yours, it's as if I can hear your voice, he told me.

# 16

A ROBIN SHOWED me the entrance to a cave that had been covered up by the underbrush. I threw a few stones into the bush to avoid any nasty surprises. There was nothing to be afraid of, not at first glance anyway. A machete would have been more useful than my Swiss Army knife. But what were a few more scratches to me anyway. I'd taken a medical flashlight with me—the doctor was easy to distract and the contents of his bag so very tantalizing. That flashlight would have been great for exploring tonsils, but it wasn't so practical for speleology. The cave descended all the way down to the river. During the war, the soldiers must have used it as their source of water through the months of fighting. The river had formed a little haven in the middle of the gorge where the fish swam confidently. I'd found my very own Robinson Crusoe desert island.

There were no paintings on the cave walls, not even any markings from the soldiers, but there was an alcove that might have, buried within it, a magnificent or terrible secret.

I dug away. Absolutely nothing inside: no bones, no weapons, not even pots or coins.

I splashed around in the river, dried myself in the sun, and went inside the alcove in my underwear. I stood upright, with my eyes closed, trying to synchronize my breathing with that of the earth.

The door to the storage room wasn't fake, nor was it hidden. Even the Lord's house has a back room. I gave it a go with my lock pick. The lock was old but it didn't moan as it surrendered to me. A saint, one that I couldn't quite identify, tried in vain to intimidate me with his mutilated arm. All the missing pipes from the organ were there. With them were enough candles for at least a thousand funerals, along with the pallium José Luis had refused to wear during the procession, which had tried the mayor's patience.

My sense of smell was warning me that the room was hiding something strange. It had to be whatever was leaning against the wall, covered by a yellowed sheet. I pulled off the sheet and gaped at the bloodstained statue of Christ. This Christ and the one on the altar had been put through different tortures. One had died a hero and the other like a lone dog fighting a pack of wolves. What was this Christ doing here? Were morbid Christs not in fashion anymore? Is that why they had banished him to limbo along with the rest of this junk?

We had it all planned out to escape one night to the old village called Belchite.

I told him what my mother had told me time and time again. At night, a dry wind would wake the voices of the dead. They'd been buried by the dozen in the oil press. The dead don't always howl though; sometimes they sing.

My grandmother's house had been occupied by soldiers who had covered the barn walls with graffiti. Of all those who wrote their name there, how many survived the war? In the little house on the hill, not far from our barren fields, there were more of the soldiers' inscriptions. One name repeated itself: César Cólera. That name, ideal for a superhero, fitting for a criminal, belonged to one of the poor wretches (one of the few who knew how to write) who wrote their names with what seemed like the handwriting of prisoners sentenced to death. My grandmother couldn't understand my anger when she ordered the builders to whitewash the barn's walls.

In the casino, behind the bottle of cognac, there was a mortar projectile that hadn't been defused. The drunks would amuse themselves with it once they'd gotten tired of playing cards. Two of them, in a sudden act of warrior's fervor, went to The Wolf's Milestone, stripped off and started to play war games. They shouted, ran, and threw stones at each other from the ditches. They almost gave the old shepherd a heart attack when he saw them. After getting his breath back, the old man took the clothes that they'd left lying around, and the warriors, now out of their trance, decided to wait till sundown to walk back home. But the people in the village had prepared a homely welcoming party; all that was missing was the marching band. They were the laughing stock of the village for months. They didn't care. They were used to being covered in glory.

In the old town of Belchite we would engage in spiritualism. He knew how to get the spirits to start talking. The twins had shown him how.

I told him to put me in contact with César Cólera. I felt that, somehow, I was connected to the unknown soldier. No problem, he told me, as long as he died there, his spirit will answer. But we have to watch our step as we could be dealing with a malicious spirit. He'd already had experiences with malicious spirits. And I can assure you that it's terrifying, he warned.

Just before arriving at the old town of Belchite, along the road known as The Sprouting Well, there was a strange door that caught the attention of those who walked past. It belonged to an isolated and derelict house that had been hit by a cannonball during the siege. It seemed like it was floating in midair. It was locked and the key was still there, no one had dared to touch it. We'd be the first to open it and cross over to the other side.

# 17

THE COBBLESTONES SEEMED like slippery skulls and my father, searching for the way out, was going the wrong way.

Isn't that your father?

After eight on Caprice Street, no one over twenty was sober. No one, that is, except the police or the dealers.

Isn't that your father?

He noticed that I'd stopped looking at my father but had asked again anyway, just to hurt me. My father stumbled from one side of the road to the other. He was spat on, pushed, kicked, and tripped up. His deafness protected him from the insults and sniggers, but he could still see the beast-like mouths and the black froth that came out of them.

I went to piss behind the cathedral and ran into him. He would have drowned in that disgusting puddle had I not dragged him out. I returned him to Caprice Street. Then I picked up an empty bottle and smashed it over the loud-mouth's head. People started to get restless. A few punches were thrown. I escaped quickly. I wasn't in the mood for more problems.

I zipped my leather jacket up to the top, set off walking with my head down and hands in my pockets. The seagulls flew over me like ghosts. A few months ago a neighbor committed suicide. His wife got on well with my aunt. They would shout over to each other from their windows and share recipes, gossip, hardships, clothespins, and the worn-out rope for the washing line. The old man had been a good guy. Unlike his wife, he didn't say much, but he would always smile at you. He wasn't euphoria incarnate, but he wasn't a grumpy old man either. He was as pale as death, I agreed with my aunt on that. He was thoughtful enough to wait for his niece to blow out the two candles on her birthday cake. The next morning he slipped out of bed, without disturbing his wife, and got a cab that took him to the other side of the city. He gave the taxi driver a generous tip and jumped down onto the train tracks from Iron Bridge. He'd been planning it for weeks, possibly months, that's for sure. Planning it so his wife and daughter would have no clue about what he was going to do. We went to Iron Bridge and continued down to the tracks to look at the fresh blood and the remains of his brain between them. Every single one of us threw up, one after another. The old man had guts, that's for sure.

# 18

*I GOT THE BEST MARKS in class again and some of the teachers congratulated me. I couldn't get out of shaking the math teacher's sweaty hand. Auntie made donuts to celebrate and they turned out delicious. It was hard to believe, but for the first time ever she didn't burn any of them. We stuffed ourselves. Auntie said afterwards that her stomach hurt, so she went to get a spoonful of fruit salts. We saved Dad a few. He works a lot and earns lots of money. Auntie says that, at this rate, we could go and move into our own house soon. I wouldn't mind being rich, why would I? As you get older you need more things, but I refuse to change neighborhoods. These are my streets, and my friends and the prettiest girls in the city live here.*

*Dad's started telling jokes. Where does he get them from? I told him the other day not to tell any of those awful jokes to his boss or he'd be risking getting fired. Auntie laughed but my Dad didn't find it funny at all. Auntie told me off for it later.*

*I haven't got proof, but I suspect that my Dad's fallen in love. That would explain his good mood, his lack of appetite,* and all that wasted cologne on the weekends. Auntie's jealous. I'm happy for him, but happier for myself. I couldn't get rid of him before. He was even more annoying than a mother, if you get what I mean.

I have a green spiral notebook. On one side I note down the things I like and on the other everything I hate. It's hard to find things I like, but there's lots of things that I hate! I surprise myself. How can anyone like the smell of burning tires? And why is it that I can't stand balloons, especially yellow ones?

The sky was cloudy again today, but you could still feel the sun's rays. They stopped me in the street and I let them stroke my face with their gloved hands for a few minutes. Afterwards, I carried on walking. The seagulls seemed more restless than usual. It's not a good sign. They're the first to notice the smell of blood.

I'm sure that the day will come when robots will rule over mankind and the world will be saved—barely, but it will be. Since robots have no hearts they're less vulnerable and therefore much less dangerous than us. Humans won't be their slaves, but their pets. Castrated and well-fed, living without ambitions, worries, only wanting to bury their toy bones, chase butterflies, and scratch at fleas. I wouldn't vote for anyone but a robot party.

Life is a cock and bull story, Auntie said as she heated up the iron. What is a cock and bull story, I asked myself. Is it one of those tales that you can't make sense of? A joke? A scam?

*She wets her finger to test if the iron is hot enough. I picture her wearing a kimono, washing clothes on the bank of an emerald river. Or burdened by a sack of screeching birds, walking across a rope bridge. She probably has so many wrinkles because she never stops ironing. If she hadn't spent all her life chained to that ironing board she'd probably have younger skin, less grey hair, better vision and posture.*

*I swear I'm going to rip the plug out and throw the iron out the window one of these days. I'll put music on and Auntie will dance to outdated songs with me. Then all her wrinkles will disappear, at least while the music keeps playing.*

Of all the letters that he wrote to his mother, this was the only one that survived the fire. I was actually surprised by his spelling: it was more than acceptable.

He was seven when he wrote his first letter. He wrote it out neatly, bought a stamp and envelope, put it in the envelope, stuck the stamp on, wrote a made-up address on it, closed the envelope and put it away. His aunt didn't want anything to do with the letters. Perhaps she could sense the diluted venom in the ink. Once he'd reached eighteen he stopped inventing fake addresses and sticking on stamps. Instead, he took them all to the beach inside a trash bag. The tide came in as the last letter finished burning and washed away the ashes. He drank a whole bottle of cheap champagne and couldn't stand up. The crabs came to my aid, he said, and he gave me the letter that he found a few days later under the carpet. There's always the odd letter that loses itself on the way. It was sealed when he gave it to me. Promise me you'll burn it and never open it. And I did so with the same conviction that you do when you make those kinds of promises.

# 19

You had to be pretty brave to open the Greenland's door and push your way through the crowd. Yet there would always be people coming in, and no one left until the night was over, or the beer was finished. They would always put the same songs on in the same order. It was quite practical, as you could always tell what time it was without having to look at your watch, and depending on the song, you knew whether to drink faster or not. The lack of oxygen and the white light leading to the great beyond made you feel as though you were in a whale's stomach. As for the toilet, you had to be pretty desperate to set foot in there. In cases of extreme necessity it was better to piss yourself. Every now and then an old woman would come empty out the cash register and disappear. All the bars on Caprice Street were the same, but none was quite like the Greenland.

It started going downhill after the Lobster started working there. You could even set foot in the toilet if you were careful enough. The old lady kept coming, but there was

barely anything there. She would dig her eyes into the
Lobster and ask him for an explanation. He would shrug
his shoulders and screw up his face.

Someone warned me that he was looking for me. I went
over to Caprice Street ready for whatever eventuality. I
didn't ask for help. Only cowards need henchmen. I pushed
the Greenland's door open with both hands. The Lobster
stopped cleaning his fingernails, stood up straight and
calmly asked me what I wanted to drink. I wished my father
could have been there to watch his son order whiskey like
a man. The Greenland's whiskey was of comparable quality
to the firewater the Comanches used when negotiating with
the Indians. He helped himself to some vodka and left the
bottles on the bar.

We drank like cowboys. The Lobster had big plans for
the future. He was crazy about motorcycles and was saving
up to buy a Harley. After crossing through Europe, he'd
conquer Asia and reach bikers' paradise: Mongolia. He told
me about the mystery surrounding Genghis Khan's tomb. A
god, Hell's first angel, he said. You could see childish sparks
of excitement in his eyes.

The old woman's apparition made him fall off his imaginary bike. She didn't even bother opening the register. That's
why I wanted to see you, he told me, as soon as the witch had
disappeared on her broomstick. I want to hire the twins, but

those two want nothing to do with me. You could convince them for me.

We would have finished off the bottle had the telephone not interrupted us. OK, on my way, don't do anything stupid, said the Lobster before hanging up. He struggled to put his jacket on and wouldn't let anyone help him. He shouted the old lady's name, but the witch must have been immersed in some poisonous potion. To hell with her, he said, and we left.

Where are we going?

I didn't ask you to follow me, he answered.

I wasn't following him to do him a favor. I was curious and it was still too early to go back home.

The Paradise was a famous breeding ground for crab lice, where the people who fell into the temptation of a dream woke up transformed into cockroaches. The receptionist looked at us over his glasses, stretched out his hand to the Lobster, shook his head, gave him a key, and went back to filling in his crossword. Stay here, the Lobster told me. There was a painting with a dead rabbit hanging from a rope. The receptionist wouldn't stop scratching his head. Boldness or daring, especially with confident disregard for personal safety, he read out loud. Eight letters. Audacity? Thanks, he said and continued chewing the end of his pencil.

The Lobster didn't come back alone. It took me a while

to recognize his sister. The neighborhood's zombie princess dropped her shoe and I followed them with the glass slipper in my hand.

The twins had one condition for the Lobster: they were in charge of the music. In less than a month the Greenland was ablaze once more. Moving across the bar like caged panthers, the twins caused delirium among the men. The guys would dig their eyes into them like they would have done with their fingers. The Lobster was busy wiping the drool off the counter. The witch ignored the twins just like they ignored her, but less tastefully.

The only song that was repeated was the one to mark the end of the night. When the first chords of "Stairway to Heaven" played, the howling stopped, the wolves grabbed their glasses, the she-wolves let their eyelids droop, and the twins, holding hands, entered into a trance. As soon as the song stopped, wolves and she-wolves abandoned the enclosure and disappeared into the night.

Truthfully, I found the Greenland's show pretty disgusting, but what else could I do if I had my own little reserved spot at the end of the bar and the tobacco and beer were free.

I would meet with the twins on Sunday nights. None of us had a driving license. They had a death wish but were better at steering than I was, and we would go around the outskirts scaring the passersby in their father's hearse. We would end up under a bridge, listening to the cars and trucks passing overhead. We smoked outside the car so as not to spoil the leather interior, and we returned it to the garage covered with mud and with the odd scratch.

# 20

AFTER THE FESTIVITIES of Saint Roch it was time to collect the pears. There were millions that summer, even if they were small and full of worms. At the end of the day my father went off with my brothers to the shop to try and get rid of the boxes, and I was left in charge of the steps and buckets. Barefoot, I dug my toes into the soil and felt roots growing out of them. The ants insisted on playing with me.

I thought you'd died, he said.

He barely showed signs of life. The flies buzzed around him like crazy.

Did the girl from the shop put up a fight? he joked as he noticed the scratches on my arm that I'd gotten from the pear tree. The girl from the shop had been dancing with a guy from the town nearby and on the second to last night of the celebrations I saw them walking to the river. Only the frogs and the August moon would know if she put up a fight or not in the all-important moment.

That jerk from the town did you a favor, he said.

What about those girls that spent the whole night crying like they were having their souls ripped from them? Are they girls or devils?

They're just cats in heat, I told him.

Our cat didn't have a name: she was just a village cat. She was confined to the barn and was the same color as the roofs, but her coat had a hint of red that gave her a distinctive look. She was always well fed, but we didn't take much notice of her. I had challenged myself to learn how to stare at her straight in the eyes; the cat, however, didn't want to teach me, or thought I was an idiot. When she wasn't careful I would toss her into the air. I'd seen in a Japanese film how the kung fu masters would teach their students how to fall on their feet by making them watch and copy the feline's movements in the air. But it wasn't true that cats always landed on their feet. She would go in and out of the barn, jumping from the neighbor's terrace. Sometimes she would go missing for weeks and come back with a swollen stomach and dirty coat, starving to death. My father wouldn't let us near the kittens. He didn't want us getting attached to them. He would put them in a sack and throw it into the pond. The pond had a strange smell and color. All the waste from the slaughterhouse and the laundromat ended up in that pond. Its water was enriched with blood, intestines, and soap. The nearby fields would produce the largest, reddest, and best tasting tomatoes in the whole region.

I told him that the kittens' meows were like heavenly music compared to the pigs' squeals from the slaughterhouse. From the moment they could smell death approaching, to the instant when the butcher slit their throats with a double-edged blade, they wouldn't stop squealing. And as they bled to death they would continue kicking and shrieking. The women would collect the streaming blood in a washtub. Their breasts would bounce around as they stirred the blood to prevent it from congealing and it would splash onto their faces and hair. After having opened the pig, the butcher with the hawk-like nose and sharp black teeth would eat a piece of liver and afterwards light a cigarette. The butt, chewed and stained with blood, was then swallowed up by the gutter.

The butcher invited us to try the raw liver and told us how there was nothing quite as sweet as it. A delicacy worthy of the gods, he'd say while licking his lips.

I didn't mention anything to him about the wind's howling during the coldest nights. It went round the whole village howling like a childless mother or like a father hunting his children down to slit their throats.

# 21

I RUBBED MY eyes. I had dried tears down my cheeks and my tongue was like sandpaper. The monsters and witches had fled, and all that was left on Caprice Street was smoke and broken glass. I looked at my boots and thought that I should really buy a new pair.

Hey, you, wake up, said one of the twins, tugging at my arm.

She took me to what seemed like a park near the cemetery. We looked for a lamppost in a deserted area. She took out a rock and a razor-blade from her pocket and whistled as she chipped away at it. Then she took out a spoon, her mother's lighter, and a syringe.

Have you got a pack of cigarettes? Give me the plastic from it.

I'd never seen her smile the way she did as her blood mixed in with the heroin.

She prepared a dose for me. I couldn't wait to try it.

All of the cells in my blood trembled sweetly.

We rolled around on the wet grass.

Are you happy?

It was my mother's voice.

Yes, mom, so happy.

The twin helped me up. We walked on all fours. I was thirsty and she told me that there was a fountain in the cemetery. We jumped over the wall and got lost among the graves. I don't know how we managed to get to the fountain. I drank all that I could and five minutes later I was throwing up even the previous night's meal in a crib-shaped grave. The twin laughed hysterically and I lost control. A thread of blood appeared on her lips. She wouldn't let me lick it off. The earth opened up beneath our feet and we stampeded out of the cemetery, jumping over walls like cartoon characters.

The swings were waiting for us. We swung over the living and the dead, almost touching the sky with the tips of our boots. The swings' chains screeched like electric guitars. The city was our birthday cake and we blew as hard as we could, but the lights wouldn't go out.

I took her back home. She didn't tell me where her sister was; I didn't bother asking either.

My aunt opened the bathroom door and there I was wrapped around the toilet. She raised her hand to her mouth to suffocate her scream that would have woken not only my father, but also the whole neighborhood.

You would throw up and then start laughing, she said. It was horrifying.

Here, have some soup, it'll do you good.

I saw the spoon in my hand tremble and I started to sweat.

My aunt fixed everything with soup or aspirin. The alphabet soup was always missing the letter U, which meant that I could never spell my name out.

Despite my complaining, my father and my aunt insisted on calling me Jesus. I didn't like "Jesus"; it sounded like a dead kid's name to me.

Some laugh like little girls when they have an orgasm, others just cry. In bed, those two whores are like day and night, said the Lobster. A weasel-like smile appeared on his face. He lit my cigarette with a gold lighter.

Have you seen my Harley? Nice, isn't it? And all thanks to you. I'll give you anything you want to repay you.

I asked for the lighter. He laughed at me through his teeth, as condescending as a newly crowned king. I turned down the whiskey he offered me and went to get some fresh air. The Harley growled from the end of the street. Everyone walking by stopped to admire it and no one dared lay a finger on it.

The motorcycle kid's reign was short-lived.

I heard that the Lobster cried like a little girl when he saw the bike of his dreams up in flames. I wasn't worried. He'd never suspect me. He'd taken me off his blacklist.

I got half a gram of happiness in exchange for the lighter. Even Genghis Khan would have cried if he'd seen his horse burn, whimpered the Lobster while wiping his nose on his sleeve. After six little sobs he told me that he loved me and I was like a brother to him. If only he knew how sick he made me, I thought to myself, he wouldn't love me so much.

# 22

WE WOULD FEED on the flies before they did the same on us, he said as he caught one in midair and put it in his mouth. He pretended to chew a few times and then spat it out. The fly was still alive, although it took some time to recover from the shock. As soon as we stopped paying attention to it, it vanished.

I didn't mention to him that my mother had been questioning me. In a farming town like mine we were never short of people trying to start fights.

My aunt sewed until her eyes fell out. She'd bought a secondhand electric sewing machine and would spend so long making gloves on it that it would often start smoking. She would try and console herself by repeating that she was worse off before, when she had to constantly pedal up and down on the Singer, like her mother had, to keep the family afloat. She would say that sewing like that was delightful. There was a pair of glasses in a handbag that we stole off an old lady.

My aunt must not have been able to see very well with them, though, because some of the gloves came out missing a finger and then others had an extra one. I don't know what was more disheartening, the noise from the sewing machine, the smell from the gloves, or my father's silence. He didn't even blaspheme anymore when the light went out and he couldn't find out if they shot the stock thieves dead, if they hung them up in a tree, or if they buried them up to their necks so that the insects and reptiles could have their fun with them.

At noon, there was an old man on every park bench in Memory Park. They begged for scraps, just like sparrows. Scraps of sunlight, that is.

What did they look at? Listen to? Think about? What did they feel? They didn't look at anything. Listen to anything. Think about anything. They didn't feel anything—not even the blood pulsating through their veins. There were statues in the cemetery that were more alive than they were.

Whenever my heart started beating too fast I'd go over to the old men for company. My friends came to rescue me. You'll turn into a fossil, they joked, and we all laughed.

Some of my friends had older brothers who had come back from doing military service. They had hair on their chests, tattoos, scars, tin medals, and crab lice. Their heroic feats of washing latrines and polishing their superiors' boots made me sick. They'd been castrated, brainwashed, and had their asses broken open without even using any Vaseline. Proud of themselves, they'd fall back into line and keep marching along with the rest of the troops.

My aunt would say that I spent too much time on the street and that there was nothing good to be learned there. She'd go on, saying that if I kept down that path I would never turn into an honest and hardworking young man. I never told her that a redskin like me would never follow the rules set out by the white man. How could I get her to understand that life in the street was just as exciting as life in the fields? She wouldn't have understood. There are certain things that the white man refuses to understand.

I listened to the murmurs in the pavement like the Indians did the whispers in the rivers. And just as they liked the smell of the purified breeze after a midday rain shower or the perfume from the pines, I liked the smell from the sewers.

# 23

MY AUNT GOT me a job. As a shop assistant, but she didn't say what kind of shop, nor could I have imagined what it would be.

My aunt couldn't sleep either. I'd hear her muttering in the kitchen—talking to herself, I presumed. I'd get up to drink a glass of water as soon as I'd hear her turn her bedroom light off and close the door. The kitchen smelled of rotting fish, but there was only a yellowed piece of chicken in the fridge and bones, eggshells, orange peels, stubbed-out cigarettes, and ash in the trashcan.

The scents and smells left behind by ghosts linger more than those from the living.

I wouldn't fall asleep until half an hour before my aunt would wake me up. By that time my father had already had breakfast and left, without shaving, with his anorak, leaving the door wide open behind him.

Did you say a prayer for me? I asked my aunt. She told me to get showered quickly and to stop talking nonsense.

I could have stayed for hours in the shower. My aunt gave me two bananas for my mid-morning snack and I stuffed them in my pockets. As I left the apartment, I pulled them out and pretended to shoot her with each of them.

Idiot, plain idiot, she'd say with all the love in the world. The bananas had turned brown and mushy, so I gave them to the watchmaker's dog. It had lost its eyesight and teeth thanks to the thousands of sugar lumps its owner had rewarded it with since he'd adopted it. It hadn't lost its sense of smell, however, as it could smell me coming from a distance. Its sickly barking worried me. Fear and hate also stir dogs' hearts.

Maybe I smelled of raw fish, like my mother, and that smell reminded him of the drunk fishermen that threw him out to sea when he was still a pup. A dog's heart holds even more rancor than a human's. The watchmaker told my aunt that he found it washed up on the beach, covered in seaweed, shaking and barking with fear. He ran over to it to scare off the hungry seagulls that were preying on him. He said that the seagulls laughed like hyenas.

Mr. Nicanor would get up early so he could have his breakfast in peace in the café on the corner. He would read the obituaries and get angry whenever an unsuspecting individual took one of the café's newspapers, preventing him from reading the names of the cemetery's newest members. He lost his temper pretty easily, but everyone in the neighborhood judged him with sympathy. He protected his honorable merchant's bald head from the rain with a Tyrolean hat and wore a blue suit, his second skin, although no one ever saw a crease or a stain on it. He was frail, big-bellied, and knock-kneed but he still managed to glide around the shop like a ballerina. Whenever a customer walked in and the bell rang, his moustache twitched amusingly. If he was dealing with a big shot, he would come out from behind the counter and humiliate himself by showering the person with praise.

There are shops that specialize in selling paraphernalia to churches just like there are those who sell office supplies and equipment to businesses. That shop was one of them, the only one, and it catered to the needs of the entire city's diocese. Nevertheless, not all of its customers were priests, friars, monks, or sacristans. Even the self-righteous came in search of scapulars, relics, rosaries, missals, bibles, crosses, candles, altar candles, and bottles of holy water from Lourdes that we filled up from the tap without the customers realizing the sacrilege.

Some priests had worm-like fingers: fat, white, and hairy ones that would drag and writhe on the counter with impatience. Then there were friars that had black slits for mouths, out of which came only monosyllables. Also, there were nuns that, no matter how hard I tried, I couldn't manage to picture naked. What would their skin smell like under all those robes? Like melted candle wax? Stagnant water? Talcum powder? Uric acid?

I clearly brought out their maternal instincts: they would try to fatten me up, rewarding me with marzipan, donuts, profiteroles, puff pastry, custard, and countless types of desserts that I would give to the watchmaker's dog to see if it would finally explode, once and for all.

Mr. Nicanor warned me not to trust their fake smiles and porcelain hands. He said that they would skin me and make cookies with my lard.

Whenever Mr. Nicanor was in a good mood he would sing church songs and cleverly insert the Devil into the lyrics. The sales had to be excellent, however, for him to be in a good mood.

> Just over in the glory land,
> I'll join the happy angel band,
> Just over in the glory land;
> Just over in the glory land,
> There with the mighty Devil I'll stand,
> Just over in the glory land.

I got bored of the porn magazines that Mr. Nicanor had

under the invoices, and instead I got hooked on reading the Bible. I read the entire thing without skipping so much as a comma, even with the tiny font and the fact that some chapters seemed like a phone book without the numbers. But there are good stories, extraordinary and spine-tingling ones that make you deeply despise humans and at the same time leave you feeling a real compassion for yourself and those around you.

I gave my aunt a rose petal rosary and my father a copy of the New Testament. I told him to read it like a western novel, and he threw the book at me and told me to go to hell.

There's only one way to read the Bible and that's drugged up, it's the only way you can understand its divinity. José Luis and I spent hours arguing about its divinity without ever reaching a conclusion.

I laughed my ass off the first time I saw him. He wiped his feet on the doormat and entered the shop. He was drenched head to toe and his umbrella was inside out. After he'd finally managed to return it to its natural state, he put it in the umbrella stand. Timidly he asked whether I had any cruets. Cruets? I said. He had to explain to me what they were and also helped me to find them, which wasn't easy because of all the dusty junk in the shop. It turned out he'd forgotten his wallet and he had to come back another day for the cruets: Mr. Nicanor had expressly forbidden me to trust anyone at all, even the Pope himself.

Whether priests have a very bad memory or an extremely good one, he told me, they only remember what they want to.

José Luis's face didn't just look pure and genuine, it radiated purity. He wore a wool sweater that seemed to weigh him down. His compassionate and hardworking mother hadn't had time to finish knitting it. Death interrupted her labor, and so the sweater had started coming undone at the sleeve and waist. He told me about a dream he'd had where he was dragging a ball of wool that would get tangled up in his legs and restrict him from moving. The martyrdom continued for years, as many as the sweater took to disintegrate.

He said that he signed up for the seminary to make his mother happy. A post-mortem type of happiness. He told me about how the priests made him sleep with his hands over the sheets and shower in under five minutes, since after the allotted time they'd cut off the hot water. I didn't believe him until I saw the seminary's silhouette and the terrifying shadows that it cast. José Luis insisted that I'd lose my mind if I ever saw it from the inside. But I'd lost my mind enough times already, so I stayed behind the gate, my heart beating wildly, watching how the darkness surrounding the place consumed my friend.

Mr. Nicanor threatened to fire me every single day for incompetence, but the days kept passing.

# 24

BARS CAN ALSO die of success, and that's exactly what happened to the Greenland. Someone, I don't know who, came up with the idea of organizing a funeral in its honor. The twins took an empty coffin from the funeral parlor. We filled it with empty bottles and took it around Caprice Street on our shoulders. Some shouted "Long live cirrhosis!" while others imitated a rooster's cry. The police, not satisfied with breaking up the funeral, also seized the coffin.

I missed the Lobster. A friend mentioned that he'd found his sister in a doorway nearby, and that it would have been pointless to call an ambulance. I felt a shiver go down my spine. I'd also thrown up in the same entrance a few times before.

The twins had always dreamed of going to London. They wouldn't forgive me for not going with them. They left without saying good-bye and called me as soon as they arrived, but I whispered to my aunt to tell them I wasn't in. A month later, they called again and my aunt forced me to answer the phone. They both spoke at once; it was impossible to understand a word of what they were saying.

They worked in a grungy hotel and basically lived off chocolate. Food is even more expensive than drugs here, they told me. And they told me how in London there were buses on fire and violent police, and that the parks seemed like cemeteries, but once the sun went down they filled up with tramps, hippies, crazy old ladies, exhibitionists, serial killers, freckled girls, insolent boys, and squirrels. They assured me that squirrels were the only friendly inhabitants in London.

Every day the twins would get hungrier, less homesick, and more in the mood to go out dancing. Whenever they started speaking to me in English, often just to tease me, I'd hang up.

One of the twins realized that she was attracted to African men and fell in love with an Arab prince. The prince wasn't too keen on white women—apparently they smelled like death to him—but the twin was always at his beck and call. She wouldn't hesitate to cross the whole of London whenever he called her. Even early one morning after he'd dreamed that the desert was talking to him and had woken up in tears. She went to him to soothe his troubles and wipe away his tears while lying next to him.

He shared an apartment with other Africans, but he told

her that he owned a palace in Jordan with palm trees, thoroughbreds, and castrated servants, and she believed him. She didn't even have enough money to buy herself food, but she had enough to give to him. In a princely manner, he'd accept the bill that reeked of death through gritted teeth and promised one day to bathe her in a bath of roses and cover her in jewelry, the day his clan retook the throne and the oil wells.

He rubbed his eyes in disbelief when he first saw the two sisters playing with the squirrels in Hyde Park and offered them a coffee, even though they were the ones who paid for it.

The guy was a two-bit drug dealer. In Soho all the waiters, drunks, police, whores, pickpockets, parasites, and other dealers, every last one of them, made fun of his blue blood. Here comes the Prince of the Sewers, they'd shout while pointing at him. He would salute them by doffing his cap, an usual gesture for a Muslim, and smiling at them like a tragic, cowardly, and unfortunate clown. But his business on the street corners of Soho flourished thanks to the twins. He told his roommates to go to hell and moved into a basement apartment that looked more like a worm-infested cake. He treated the two twins like dirt. You stink of dead dogs, he'd tell them whenever he wanted to get rid of them, and they would call me from a phone booth yelping and sobbing to me. I preferred not to ask them where they would sleep that night, or if they were planning to sleep at all.

I wasn't prepared to suffer for them. They could always kill the Arab, cut him to pieces, and throw him in the Thames. They could have always come back home, although they never considered that as an option.

Every now and then they would send me photos. Photos of squirrels dyed blue, concert photos, or police officers with pig-like faces beating protesters with their nightsticks. They would never take photos of each other, and that got to me; they always used to fight over who would be in photos.

They no longer insisted on me going to visit them in London, and that wasn't because they'd lost hope of getting me to leave the neighborhood.

Any time I saw a hearse pass by it reminded me of them and how we used to kill time on Sundays, riding around in their father's car. I'd say that if things ever turned out for the worse, we could always open our own funeral parlor. We could have called it "Stairway to Heaven." We'd honor the dead with black flowers and install small speakers inside the coffins to guarantee them the maximum comfort possible.

I didn't recognize anyone in the disco. The twins took a few gulps of their drinks and headed to the dance floor. They showed the same indifference that gladiators did when they battled the furies brought from the far corners of the earth. The crowd let them through and the twins looked at them from the corners of their eyes, smiling but without moving their lips. The moment they stepped onto the dance floor the music stopped, and after a few moments of silence, a sticky kind of silence, the horns of Jericho or the Apocalypse started to sound, and they threw their long, dirty hair against the light looking like they were charging from its electricity. To start with they moved as if they were being whipped, but later on they were the ones lashing out in every direction, possessed by some evil spirit. Death doesn't wait long to make its appearance. It was dressed like a saint but with the make-up of a prostitute. Still, you could tell who it was—anyone with eyes can recognize it. The twins were on guard, even if they said differently. The lights and music become frantic whenever Death steps onto the dance floor. It's a professional, it knows how to do its job and enjoys doing it too. Its demeanor isn't to act like a predator. The twins could dance long enough to wear Death out, but the disco had a closing hour. I went to the men's room, I couldn't hold on any longer, and when I came back the lights were off as well as the music, and the twins had disappeared along with Death. I collected my jacket from the coatroom and saw the twins' jackets still hanging there. I asked the girl to give them to me, but she said she couldn't. The vile morning light awaited me out in the street.

# 25

THE BELLS WENT crazy. No one was home, not my father, mother, or brothers. I heard cars outside and rushed to the kitchen window—it was the Land Rovers of the police. My neighbor, holding a basket of eggs in her arms, stayed glued to the chicken pen door. The eggs trembled in the basket. I went up to the roof and climbed across my neighbors' houses until I reached the priest's. I'd take him to my cave, they'd never find him there. I saw his black glasses abandoned on the table. I didn't need to see any more.

My mother ran up the stairs, clearly upset. I was sprawled out on the sofa, my head buried in between the leather seats.

Don't beat yourself up about it, he'll turn up, she said, and I began to relax.

The officers were looking for my uncle; he'd gotten lost on the mountain.

I started laughing and my mother stared at me with one of those motherly looks that manage to combine disbelief, shock, and resignation all in one.

My uncle had gone to the mountain that morning with

a wheelbarrow. He'd stopped to talk to someone for a few minutes and said that he was going to fetch some rocks. My uncle was over eighty years old and had always had a screw loose. It ran in the family.

They called him Cucumber Head. If you'd seen him take his beret off as he entered the church then you'd understand that the villagers weren't exaggerating.

They were waiting for the helicopter to arrive. The police sergeant had told the mayor, and the mayor had told my father. Would it be like one of those helicopters from the Vietnam War?

They found my uncle before the helicopter arrived. He'd fallen into a ditch and had spent the night purging himself of all his sins. The doctor bandaged his ankle and congratulated him on his idiocy.

Everyone wondered why he was looking for rocks.

My uncle wasn't much of a talker. He trusted me however. Whenever he received a letter, or needed to write something, he'd come to me for help. He was the one who gave me my first typewriter: a red Olivetti. He went all the way to Zaragoza on the bus to buy it for me. I looked after it as if it were a living being.

What went through your head when you were stuck in that ditch? Did you see the Devil? Did you speak with him? What did you talk about?

He continued to go to the mountain looking for rocks

with his wheelbarrow. He'd pile them up in front of his house. Ordinary rocks of every shape and size.

People get strange things stuck in their heads, my mother would say.

I explained what the difference between a swift and a swallow was. I told him that, like robins, swifts had red breasts that had been dyed with the blood of Christ on the cross.

You talk like an old man, he said.

While the swallows and the swifts ate, screeched, and danced, we stacked sunflower seeds on top of each other in a pile, linked together smoke rings, and envied the sexual spontaneity of flies.

I saw a punk bird this morning, he said, with an insanely colorful crown.

I told him it must have been a hoopoe. A bird as glamorous as it was annoying and foul smelling. Like stink bombs, but with wings.

So they're real punks then, he said laughing.

I'd rather die a coward than live like one, as one of his favorite punk rock bands sang.

He was fortunate enough to meet the singer after a concert in a squat. The singer, a troubled addict, started a brutal fight which he didn't think twice about running from as soon as he heard the clicking of switchblades. We shared a needle in a doorway, he told me, and we laughed at how cowardly our shadows must have looked.

# 26

LOOK, HE SAID.

It was a dead bird. It had fallen from the sky. He threw it onto the roof knowing that the cats wouldn't eat it.

Pain tells me that I'm still alive.

At night, José Luis would come into my room and approach my bed to check that I hadn't stopped breathing and then sit in the dark to watch over me.

Last night I told him that if Christ had been a true hero, he wouldn't have accepted the cross of obedience. José Luis shifted about uncomfortably in his seat and mumbled to himself under his breath.

He thinks that I should confess to him, but I don't think so.

My father cried tears of blood, like Christ, but I'm not going to cry. The twins would never let me forget it.

Whatever my aunt wouldn't dare say to my father's face when he was alive, she said about him after his death.

She continued to wake up early and fry eggs, which she ended up eating herself. The ghosts didn't like fried eggs and neither did I. She also continued to sew gloves that no one bought from her and the apartment filled up with those ridiculous and menacing gloves.

She filled up her purse just so I could empty it again. I took her sewing machine, iron, television, and the rose-petal rosary. She would have let me rip her eyes out, or even done it herself, had I asked her to.

It's only now that I realize that my aunt would have made a great biblical character, unlike me and my father, who were more like cartoon characters.

He was dressed too elegantly to be a police officer. He wore a striped suit and expensive shoes and smoked like a Hollywood actor. Our eyes met and he coolly diverted his attention.

I couldn't wait to go to bed. I was hoping that my aunt had gone shopping or to church. Ever since my father's death, at least once a week, she'd go out with three or four friends, all widows. Sitting down to pray, they'd finish the beads on their rosaries, go to the bakery, and then play a game of whist. My aunt didn't care that they cheated.

They had probably coughed up enough already and my aunt and mother were exhausted, crushed. Why so much suffering when joy and hurt go down the same drain, my aunt would say. My boots started to stick to the floor tiles. I kicked them off and sprawled out on my father's armchair. I lit a cigarette and let it burn out between my fingers. My father's spirit swirled around the room. I grabbed at the air trying to capture him.

It wasn't the pain in her anguished eyes, her pleading hands, or her babbling that hurt me. It was her beauty. She was prettier than I had imagined, infinitely more than the fishmonger's wife.

I stood up and walked over to her, drawn by the light reflecting off her hair. I sniffed at her. You don't smell like raw fish, I said and returned to slouching in my father's armchair.

She wanted to say something, but her cry was suffocated. She went out leaving her handbag behind her. I'd only seen bags like those in the shop windows in the center of town.

We didn't have time to open it. Five minutes later the bell rang. It was the Hollywood actor. A polite and elegant man. I was happy for her.

# 27

WE WATCHED THE gaping ghost suffering as it realized it wasn't able to smoke. José Luis paced up and down with his hands behind his back, as though he were handcuffed. I was sitting on the roof with my legs dangling off the edge. Come with me, he said suddenly. I followed him into the kitchen. He'd taken the brush, roller, and tins of paint out again, but it didn't look like he was in the mood for painting. Neither was I, so I didn't bother offering to give him a hand.

The room still smelled of sulfur. The bulb hanging from the ceiling didn't go on, but there was a lamp on the bedside table. The cross that took center stage over the iron bed was hung upside down. José Luis smiled as he noticed it and, after giving it a kiss, he put it back to normal.

He took a huge pile of papers out from under the bed. He told me how his hands never shook when he was drawing. I swore, hand on the Bible, that I'd burn all of them, but that I could keep the ones I liked. He'll forgive me and so will God.

All the drawings featured a completely naked Christ, crowned with thorns. Christ playing the guitar, a Fender Telecaster, the Devil's favorite. Christ massacring Jews with a machine gun. Christ chopping off a Roman's head with his own sword, and another Roman soldier lying on the ground with a lance through his chest. Christ fighting a pigeon with bull horns. Christ dancing with rats. Christ dancing with fairies, witches, and nuns. Christ on horseback with a revolver in each hand, shooting into the air. Christ turning his back to a broken down woman in tears. Christ hacking down a forest of crosses with a Viking axe. Christ battling Spider-Man. Christ going up against King Kong. Christ fighting Popeye. Christ taking on Bruce Lee. Christ running after the Road Runner. Christ preaching to a pack of wolves. Christ preparing to shave in front of a mirror. Christ brushing his teeth. Christ shaking hands with Groucho Marx. Christ shaking hands with Gorbachev. Christ with a chicken leg, chewing with his mouth full. Christ with donkey ears. Christ about to shoot John Lennon. Christ staking Dracula. Christ in front of another beat-up Christ. Christ among those shot in the *Third of May.* Christ blowing a bubble with chewing gum. Christ in a soccer goal. Christ smoking a huge joint. Christ bowling. Christ pissing against a wall with LONG LIVE ME written on it. Christ sitting in a puddle of urine. Christ cutting his toenails.

Christ blow-drying his long, dirty hair. Christ among trash bags and excited cats. Christ preaching to monkeys. Christ clutching a canary in his fist. Christ with a bare umbrella under a black rain cloud. Christ in the bath. Christ sharing a needle with Donald Duck. And then again with Peter Pan. Christ with hypnotized eyes. Christ blowing out candles on a birthday cake. Christ watering carnivorous plants with a hose. Christ slitting a lamb's throat. Christ trying to make a beer last. Christ trying to swallow a sword. Christ juggling ketchup bottles. Christ pole-vaulting. Christ pulling rabbits out of a hat. Christ trying to run away from the moon. Christ throwing lightning bolts. Christ preaching to penguins. Christ with his own head in his hands. Christ in the lotus position. Christ bored on a deserted island. Christ swinging over the abyss. Christ with a halo of flies, speaking to a child with Dumbo-like ears.

We burned them all in the garden. The wind blew angrily and caused the ashes to look like a flock of flaming birds, scattering on the rooftops. The wind took the ashes away with it.

It was getting dark. José Luis told me to go home. They'll be waiting for you to start dinner.

# 28

THE BED IN the execution room in Texas Prison is shaped like a cross. The condemned are tied down with straps and looking up at the ceiling. Hanging from the ceiling is a microphone that records their last words; messages, good-byes, and cries into the void that can be found on the prison's website.

In the last thirty years, in this prison alone, they've cruci-fied more than five hundred. Whites, blacks, Hispanics, and a few women. Thanks to the lethal injection, death comes to them in gentle waves. In Pilate's time, they'd break the legs of those on the cross, not only to speed up their death, but also to make sure that they couldn't be given a burial: those mutilated souls weren't worthy enough to receive a proper one.

Those on death row lovingly say good-bye to their moth-ers; rarely do they mention anything about their fathers.

There are plenty who believe that Jesus will welcome them with open arms.

Pedro Martínez was executed in 2006. Convicted of killing a police officer who pulled him over for speeding. His final words were: "Only the rats and the sky survive, and today's as good as any to die."

# 29

THEY'VE PAVED THE road leading to the cemetery, but I walked down there just as I used to, following the cliff's edge, just to put myself through a little suffering. I would often come here alone, at all hours, even during the night. I thought that it was one of those places where the living and the dead meet. It was anything but boring, that's for sure.

I didn't feel like going up to the chapel to have a look at the town from high up. It's depressing seeing all the collapsed roofs.

I could have sworn that the birds were happy to see me—that is, if I didn't know that they only sang for the dead and ignored the living.

A small cloud with rabbit's feet chased a larger one with a dragon's tail.

The only things that grow in this town are crosses. However, a few flowers have started to grow between the rocks. They're the kind of flowers that won't let you touch them and don't look at you like other flowers do, trying to get your attention.

Every year there are more rocks. The scorpions will be happy. Even the dead will be happy with the gleaming dust that shines on the cemetery walls.

In a western film a cowboy with the face of a gangster said:

"Why are people so afraid of the dead? The dead are my only friends, because one can only trust the dead in foul times like these. Sure they smell bad, but then so do the living."

There's something buried on this path that belongs to me. I buried it here myself, I'm sure. But I can't remember what it was or where I buried it. I'll go insane if the dead don't help me find it.

There used to be thyme growing everywhere. They say that thyme flowers ward off nightmares.

I'd prefer not to look over the edge of the cliff and see what's at the bottom. It's not that I'm scared of seeing the child I once was, circled by vultures; I'm afraid that if I look down, something will look back at me.

As a child I used to dream that I was able to fly. It's the only thing that I miss from my childhood. Those dreams that didn't obey the laws set by reality.

I wouldn't even have to move my arms to fly. Actually, instead of flying, I would just elevate like a balloon and, high above, laugh down at my enemies, who thought that I'd made myself vanish with my magic powers.

But I didn't even feel safe in the air. I could have ended up trapped in the claws of a she-eagle.

I threw a stone over the edge and it took an eternity to reach the bottom.

You think that what you're hearing are your footsteps and the beating of your own heart. It doesn't even occur to you that it might be someone else's footstep or someone else's heartbeat that you're hearing.

At the end of the path we shook hands. He stayed behind, whistling to himself, and we soon lost sight of each other.

JULIO JOSÉ ORDOVÁS was born in 1976 in Zaragoza, a city in which he still resides. He is a contributor to the supplement *Cultura in La Vanguardia* and the magazines *Clarin* and *Turia*. He has published seven books.

CHRISTIAN MARTIN-ROFFEY works in Information Technology in Dublin, Ireland. This is his first book-length translation to be published in English.